This book belongs to:

- - - - - - - - - - - - - - - - - - - -

For the wonderful Wayne Winstone and his words of wisdom.

With love.

K.S.

Sir Charlie Stinky Socks would like to donate 10% of the royalties from the sale of this book to Naomi House Children's Hospice.

EGMONT
We bring stories to life

First published in Great Britain 2010
by Egmont UK Limited
239 Kensington High Street
London W8 6SA

Text and illustrations copyright © Kristina Stephenson 2010
All rights reserved
Kristina Stephenson has asserted her moral rights

ISBN (HB) 978 14052 4827 3
ISBN (PB) 978 14052 4828 0

1 3 5 7 9 10 8 6 4 2

A CIP catalogue record for this title
is available from the British Library

Printed and bound in Malaysia

Sir Charlie Stinky Socks

and the Really DREADFUL Spell

Kristina
Stephenson

EGMONT

Once upon a misty morning, from the top of a twisty-wisty **beanstalk**, *Someone* was looking down . . .

. . . on to a tall, tall tower (with a pointy roof) in the middle of . . .

… a Magical Forest.

It was the day after a little Princess's party and everyone was happy there, when, **suddenly** – without any warning – **Someone …**

… cast a *spell!*

And over the Princess,
her favourite monster, and
a wily witch with a watch
(oh and everyone else in this magical world),
a **stony** silence fell!

Now...

...only a power mightier than magic
could break this *dreadful spell*
(*if* such a power could reach the tower
before the sands of time r a n o u t!).

But the only power that was strong enough was twenty
leagues from there - in the boots of a knight who'd
been at the party and was making his way back home.

Oh no!

Further away from the tower
went the power *until...*

... Sir Charlie Stinky Socks stopped. *Phew!*

The bold, brave knight, and his faithful
cat, Envelope, wanted a bite to eat.
So Sir Charlie took out a slice of cake
(a piece he had brought from the Princess's party)
and with one quick flick of his
trusty sword he –

Hang on a minute!
Hold this story!

Where *was* his
trusty sword?

It was back in the tower, at the bottom of the stairs –
where he'd left it after the party.

Gadzooks!

"Never mind," said Sir Charlie. "I suppose lunch will just have to wait."
And he rallied his faithful (famished) cat and
mounted his groaning grey mare.

Clip clop, clip clop,

clippety clippety clop!

Back to the forest and the
tall, tall tower rode
Sir Charlie and his cat.

Oh, and his mighty power
went with him
(along with some wiggly woos).

Good job too!

For in the tall, tall tower
(with the pointy roof) time was . . .
running out!

The *mists* grew *mistier*.
Murkier too!

And some worrying signs in
the road suggested the
gallant knight
might be . . .

. . . *lost!*

WHERE'S THE TOWER?

HAVEN'T THE FOGGIEST!

Oh no !
Deep woe !
Which way to go?

Sir Charlie was about to find out.
For through that muddlesome
murky mist,
he saw **Someone**
heading his way.

Aha, thought Sir Charlie, a **mysterious stranger** pulling a heavy load!
Just the thing for a knight to meet at a moment such as this.

"Good morrow, *stranger*," said Sir Charlie. "Whither do you wander?"

"Over the hills and far away," said the **mysterious stranger,** "with the rubbish I collected from a tall, tall tower in the middle of a *Magical Forest.* They had a **rip-roaring party** — you see —

with **guests**
            and a **cake**
                        and **balloons!**
And when the party was over," snorted the *stranger,* "I had to . . .

. . . sort out the mess!"

"What luck, my fine fellow!" said Sir Charlie, "that you and I should meet. For *I*, Sir Charlie Stinky Socks, am trying to get *back* to that tower - I need to fetch my trusty sword, so I can cut up this cake for lunch."

"*Hmmm*," said the **stranger** with a sneaky smile, "then you'd better not delay. If you'll let me share your lunch with you, I'll . . . *show you the quickest way!*"

Sir Charlie harnessed his hungry horse to the stranger's cart full of rubbish and set off again through the **murky mists** on his journey back to the tower . . .

trit trot, trit trot, *humpity lumpity bump!*

. . . paying little heed to the worrying signs and the stranger's sneaky smile and not even *knowing* that in the tall, tall tower, time was . . .

r
u
n
n
i
n
g out!

At last they
were back in the
Magical Forest
where things looked . . .

decidedly different!

For in front of our troupe of tiring travellers was . . .

So was the cat,
the horse
and the cart . . . (and the power to break the spell!)

Well . . . a quick-witted knight, on a cart full of rubbish, wouldn't watch this happen.
No, no!

He'd rummage around in that jumble of junk while he worked out what to do.
Could you?

In no time at all, in that **burbling bog** . . .

. . . a bubbling, burbling bog!
Yuck!

There was no way round it,
no way through it and no way now to go back!
Because by some horrible hand of fate
this bog was . . .

. . . **all around!**

Envelope *moaned*.
The grey mare *groaned*.

All hope of lunch was
s i n k i n g.

. . . clever Sir Charlie did!
Yippee!
How odd then that the **mysterious**
stranger lost his sneaky smile while . . .

slappety squelch,
slappety squelch,
splodge, splodge, splodge!

. . . Sir Charlie Stinky Socks
(and his mighty power) drew closer
to the tall, tall tower. The knight ignored
the worrying signs and the anxious
wiggly woos and followed the lead of the
mysterious stranger who guided them
thoughtfully through

that **burbling bog**

and the *murky mist*

to the middle of . . .

. . . a **monstrous maze!**
Oh my!

Now - where in the world
did *that* come from?

And would our band of weakening
wanderers work out a way to get through–
at least before they fainted with hunger
(and the sands of time ran out)?

Yikes!

Envelope sighed as the grey mare tried and
all too soon gave up, while
the **mysterious stranger**
(who'd found his sneaky smile again)
tittered through his teeth.

But so did
Sir Charlie
Stinky Socks
who *liked* to be
put to the test.

And with nothing but rubbish and imagination, he . . .

. . . found the way out of that **monstrous** maze back to the tall, tall tower and the *twisty-wisty beanstalk* and . . .

. . . **a dragon made of stone!**

What?

Not coughing out fire, nor belching out smoke?

Just sad . . . and silent . . . and still; like each of the creatures at the bottom of the tower – all under a *dreadful spell.*

But who could have cast it?
Well, can't you guess?

Yes! Yes! Yes!

First there was the mist, then there
was the bog and of course
the **monstrous maze.**

All together the worrying signs pointed to
. . .

Terrible piercing **spikes** they were,
pushing Sir Charlie back - *back* to
the farthest limb of the *beanstalk*
where he teetered on the brink.

"**Think!**" said Sir Charlie Stinky Socks.
And he didn't need to think *twice*.

With a **wooshity thwack** of his trusty sword he -

Hang on a second!
Have you forgotten?

He didn't *have* his sword!

That lusty blade was *inside* the tower
while the desperate knight was . . .

. . . *without.*
Nooooo!

Envelope *gasped.*

The grey mare *gulped.*

But Sir Charlie didn't think thrice . . .

How unfortunate then that
    he dropped those socks as he
        clambered into the tower.

. . . he kicked off his boots,
whipped off his socks and
wafted them in the air!

Wow! The powerful pong from those
pungent stockings . . .

. . . withered the thorns away!

**Hey
hey!**

"Ha ha," said Sir Charlie. "My stinky socks are mightier than the sword!"

... the **mysterious stranger**, roaring with laughter at the top of the tower where time was a l m o s t o u t !

Up the *twisty-wisty beanstalk* scrambled Sir Charlie Stinky Socks – right to the top of the tall, tall tower where . . .

. . . *something* made him **STOP!**

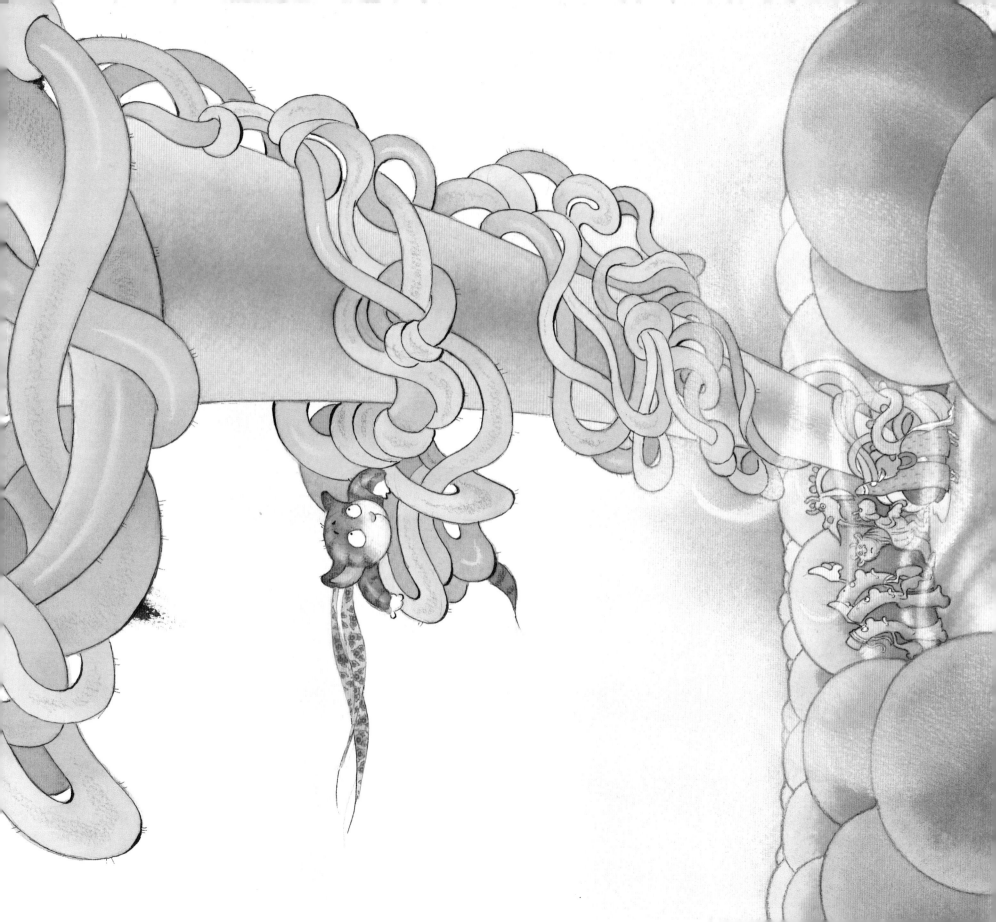

Three stone figures –
silent and still – stood
in the middle of
the room where the
mysterious stranger
(with the sneaky smile)
revealed what he
really was.

A wizard, of course - who'd been in disguise -
now *that* would explain a lot!
"So! Little Stinky Socks!" he boomed at Sir
Charlie. "You made it to the tower! You got through
my **mist**, my **bog**, my **maze**, and even my **piercing thorns**. But
here, my fearless, foolish friend, you'll meet your match in **me** -
the most powerful Wizard that ever there was from the
top of the twisty beanstalk.

I have bewitched the
creatures in the forest and your
friends in this tall, tall tower."

"Why?" said Sir Charlie to the wicked wizard.
"What did *they* do to *you?*"

"They had a **rip-roaring party**
So I turned them all to **stone**
can turn them back
than magic can
get it?" sneered
"That power
but *they*
of the
is about
out!

of course, but they didn't invite *me!*

– see? – and not even *you* my brave little knight again. Because, only a power mightier break this **dreadfull spell**. And don't you the wicked wizard. **is in your socks . . .** are at the bottom tower and time to run **Ha!"**

No point arguing with an angry wizard – at least not at a time like this. If Sir Charlie were going to save his friends he'd have to . . .

. . . take **the blame!**

"I brought everyone to the Princess's party,"
said the honest knight. "If anyone here should
be turned to stone, I think
it should be me."

How tragic then for Sir Charlie Stinky Socks
that the Wizard was quick to agree.

He lifted up his fearsome wand and pointed it at Sir Charlie.

But wait!

What was that coming in through the window?

A faithful, fearless cat, no less!
Who got to the top of the
tall, tall tower just as the
Wizard cast his *spell* . . .

By tea-time there was laughter in the tall, tall tower as the sun broke through the *mists*. Sir Charlie took out the piece of cake he'd brought from the princess's party and with a **choppity chop** of his trusty sword he–

Hold your horses!

(And the tea!)

Even with his sword – how could Sir Charlie make one piece of cake go among so many?

Unless . . . **oh yes** . . .

. . . the Wizard was
sorry and wanted
to make amends.

"Behold," said Sir Charlie, "my stinky socks may hold a mighty power but *a heart that is true and a friend who is faithful are mightier things by far.*"

Envelope leaped in front of Sir Charlie to take the terrible blow.

At that self-same second, in the tall, tall tower . . .

. . . the sands of time ran out!

But instead of the cat
being turned to stone,
something incredible happened.

The *dreadful spell* was broken!

With a **wooshity thwack** of
his magic wand the
cake became . . .

. . . a feast! **Hurrah!**

And that was that in the tall, tall tower,

A happily ever after!

Sir Charlie Stinky Socks hugged his cat and patted his good grey mare.

"'Twas a job well done!" he said to them.

"Now – are you ready for *another* adventure?"

THE END?